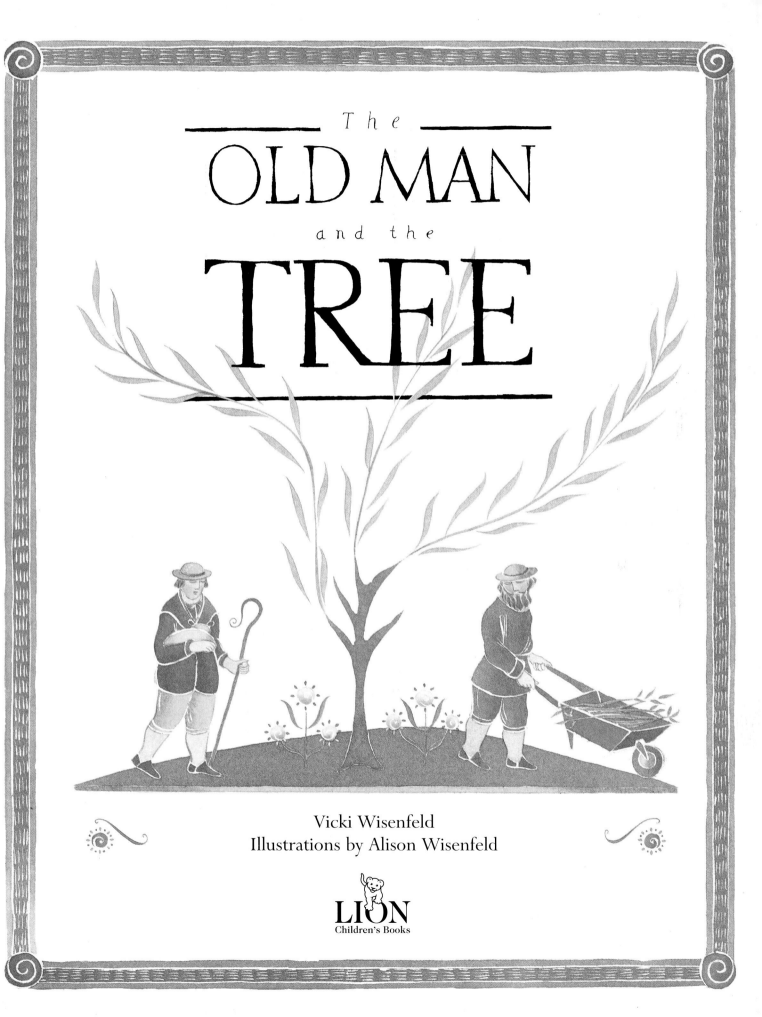

The OLD MAN and the TREE

Vicki Wisenfeld

Illustrations by Alison Wisenfeld

LION
Children's Books

Once there was a willow tree. It grew near the cottage of an old craftsman called Walter. Each time Walter cut down one of its five branches it grew back again! But only if whatever he made was used kindly towards others.

Over the years the tree never failed to grow.

Until one spring when there was a near disaster.

It began on a Monday. An old woman spotted the
willow tree and called out, 'Old man, will you weave
me a new basket?'

Walter replied, 'Gladly. But remember this: use it kindly, sharing and caring, helping and loving others. The tree depends on this.'

So the old man made a strong and sturdy basket. And the woman carried it on her way to market.

After she had filled it with delicious bread, shiny apples and cheeses, she met a poor man begging in the street.

But, forgetting the old man's words, the greedy woman did not listen to his hungry cries.

Suddenly she felt the basket shake and shiver,
toss and turn. Branches and leaves sprouted!
But on the tree no new shoot grew.

On Tuesday a young boy saw the willow tree
and cried out, 'Old man, will you make me a bat?'

Walter replied, 'Gladly. But remember this: use it kindly, sharing and caring, helping and loving others. The tree depends on this.'

So the old man shaped and sanded a pale smooth bat. And the boy grabbed it and ran off to play.

In the match that day he was the star player.
Everyone marvelled at his skill and talent.

But, forgetting the old man's words, the proud
boy started to boast that he was the greatest.

Suddenly he felt the bat whirl and wheel
around and about. Branches and leaves sprouted!
But on the tree no new shoot grew.

On Wednesday a farmer saw the willow tree and
shouted out, 'Old man, will you make me a fence
to keep my sheep safe?'

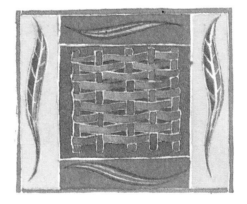

Walter replied, 'Gladly. But remember this: use it kindly, sharing and caring, helping and loving others. The tree depends on this.'

So the old man wove a tall fence which the farmer bundled up and took to his farm.

Counting his sheep that night the farmer noticed that one was missing.

'Too bad,' the lazy farmer thought, forgetting the old man's words. And he shut in the rest of the sheep.

Suddenly he saw the fence strain and stretch,
forwards and backwards. Branches and leaves
sprouted!

But on the tree no new shoot grew.

On Thursday a fisherman came past and saw the willow tree. He called out, 'Old man, will you make me a coracle?'

Walter replied, 'Gladly. But remember this: use it kindly, sharing and caring, helping and loving others. The tree depends on this.'

So with deft fingers and strong hands the old man constructed a coracle. And the fisherman carried it on his shoulders to the river.

That day the fisherman hauled in so many fish that his coracle was soon full and brimming over.

But, forgetting the old man's words, the wasteful fisherman rowed home, leaving most of them lying on the river-bank.

Suddenly he felt the coracle jump and jerk as it
flung itself around! Branches and leaves sprouted!
But on the tree no new shoot grew.

On Friday a passing merchant noticed the willow
tree and asked, 'Old man, will you sell me some logs
to keep my family warm?'

Walter replied, 'Gladly. But remember this: use them kindly, sharing and caring, helping and loving others. The tree depends on this.'

So the old man sawed and chopped a pile of logs and the merchant carted the firewood home.

That evening the merchant heard a knock on his door and a voice cried out, 'Help! I need shelter!' But, forgetting the old man's words, the selfish merchant replied, 'Go away! Don't bother me.'

Suddenly he saw the logs totter and tumble,
heave and thrash! Branches and leaves sprouted!
But on the tree no new shoot grew.

On Saturday Walter looked at his willow tree.
Now there were no branches left! He had to find
the people who had harmed the tree.

So the old man left his cottage and set off down the road. He hadn't gone very far when he found the old woman. Together they went on to the village to find the boy, across the open fields to find the farmer, down to the river to find the fisherman, and off to the town to find the merchant.

Then they all followed Walter home to see what was wrong.

When they saw the willow tree they were sorry and wept. They cried so much that their tears ran like a river into a big pool of water around the tree.

But Walter was a good, kind man. He could see that they really were sorry, so he forgave them for their thoughtlessness.

Suddenly an extraordinary thing happened.
Five new shoots appeared on the willow tree!
Everyone danced with joy and promised Walter
that from then on they would be kind to others.

On Sunday Walter rested in the shade of his tree
and smiled happily to himself, dreaming of all the
things he would make for his new friends.

Published by
Lion Publishing plc
Sandy Lane West, Oxford, England
www.lion-publishing.co.uk
ISBN 0 7459 4231 8
Lion Publishing
4050 Lee Vance View, Colorado Springs,
CO 80918, USA
ISBN 0 7459 4231 8

First edition 2000
10 9 8 7 6 5 4 3 2 1 0

A catalogue record for this book is available
from the British Library

Library of Congress CIP data applied for

Typeset in 20/28 Lapidary 333 BT
Printed and bound in Malaysia